# NOT NOW,
# BERNARD

1 3 5 7 9 10 8 6 4 2

Text and illustrations © 1980 David McKee

David McKee has asserted his right under the Copyright,
Designs and Patents Act, 1988
to be identified as author and illustrator of this work

First published in the United Kingdom 1980
by Andersen Press
First published in Mini Treasures edition 1996
by Red Fox
Random House, 20 Vauxhall Bridge Road, London SW1V 2SA

Random House Australia (Pty) Limited
20 Alfred Street, Milsons Point, Sydney,
New South Wales 2061, Australia

Random House New Zealand Limited
18 Poland Road, Glenfield,
Auckland 10, New Zealand

Random House South Africa (Pty) Limited
PO Box 2263, Rosebank 2121, South Africa

Random House UK Limited Reg. No. 954009

A CIP catalogue record for this book
is available from the British Library

ISBN 0 09 972541 X

Printed in Singapore

# DAVID McKEE

# NOT NOW, BERNARD

## Mini Treasures

RED FOX

"Hello, Dad," said Bernard.

"Not now, Bernard," said his father.

"Hello, Mum," said Bernard.

"Not now, Bernard," said his mother.

"There's a monster in the garden and it's going to eat me," said Bernard.

"Not now, Bernard," said his mother.

Bernard went into the garden.

"Hello, monster," he said to the monster.

The monster ate Bernard up, every bit.

Then the monster went indoors.

"ROAR," went the monster behind
Bernard's mother.

"Not now, Bernard," said Bernard's mother.

The monster bit Bernard's father.

"Not now, Bernard," said Bernard's father.

"Your dinner's ready," said Bernard's mother.

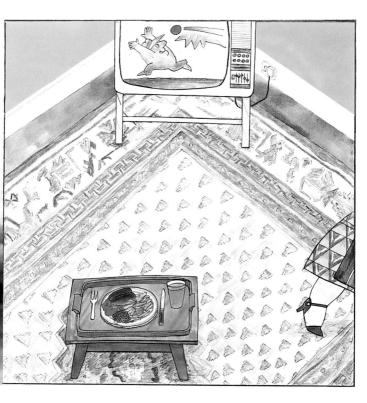

She put the dinner in front of the television.

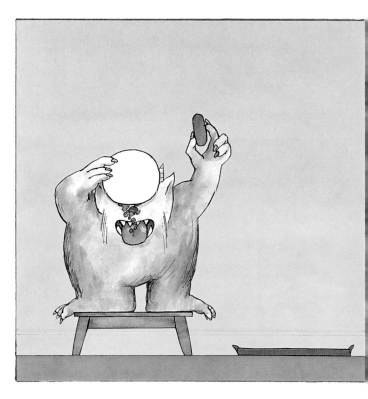

The monster ate the dinner.

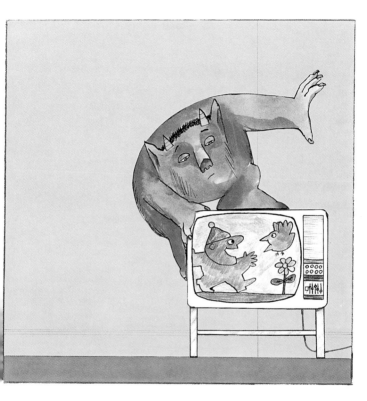

Then it watched the television.

Then it read one of Bernard's comics.

And broke one of his toys.

"Go to bed. I've taken up your milk," called Bernard's mother.

The monster went upstairs.

"But I'm a monster," said the monster.

"Not now, Bernard," said Bernard's mother.